RUTHLESS

Ruthless
Written by Natalie L. Gamble
Copyright © 2018 by Snow Publishing
Published by Snow Publishing LLC

This story is a work of fiction. Any resemblances to actual events, real people, living or dead, organizations, establishments or locales are products

Edited by Nina
Cover Design by Michael Horne

Prologue

	She rolled her eyes heavenward and sighed at the phone as Cedric continued to plead his case. She didn't want to hear it, he was two hours late and carefully laid plans were ruined. He was done. Three strikes?! No, she wasn't having it you got one and he had used it. His replacement was in route, Devon would be there in 15 minutes. "Cedric, I don't care, why are you still talking it's a wrap!" He sounded like a pitiful puppy as he whined.

	"Rave please I had to work late damn!" Raven tossed her hair over her shoulder and laughed.

"I don't care if Obama is calling you to service! No call, no show, no Raven that's why your ass is sitting on the curb bye Cedric!" She pressed 'end on her phone and grabbed her makeup bag. "He got it twisted, working late? How is that my problem?" She studied her reflection in the mirror and smirked "I look too damn good to wait." Raven was beautiful, soft long dark brown hair, that hung between her shoulder blades, blue green eyes that drew you in or cut you deep depending on her mood. Her milk chocolate skin was flawless with or without makeup and her curves she inherited from her mother stopped men in their tracks wherever she went. Making sure her makeup was on point she passed the next few minutes blocking

Cedric out of her life after sending his last-ditch effort phone call to voicemail. He wasn't the first nor would he be the last to be cut from 'Team Raven' she could make a man a 'has been' with a few finger swipes.

Her doorbell rang and Devon stood there smiling when she opened the door. "Hey beautiful I'm glad you called." Devon wasn't her first pick but he was fine as hell so she'd overlook some of his flaws. She smiled as he handed her a bouquet of roses. She laid the flowers on the table by her front door after she sniffed them briefly. He frowned as she grabbed her purse and jacket. "Aren't you going to put those in water?" One carefully sculpted eyebrow arched.

"I will when we get back, the AC is on is that a problem Devon?" She watched his nostrils flare, his face reddens, his jaw jump as his teeth clenched.

"No Raven it's fine." Her ever present smirk returned.

"Good let's go." She smiled to herself thinking. "Nobody told you to bring me damn flowers anyway, I mean who wants something beautiful that dies anyway?"

Most people who 'knew' Raven couldn't stand her, they felt she was ungrateful, self-centered, and in a word, a Bitch. She didn't care. She felt she got what she deserved and those who didn't like it were jealous. Raven had traveled all around the world, rocked only the newest and hottest clothes, bags, and shoes. Her jewelry collection put Jared's to shame. All this and it was never on Raven's dime. Raven hadn't paid for so much as a sandwich on a date since she was 16. Now at 32 she could pay her own way if she chose to, Raven was very successful and wealthy. Her house and cars and those of her parents were all paid for by Raven.

Devon walked quietly in front Raven opening and closing his fists all the way back to his car. He slid in the driver's seat reached over and unlocked and opened the passenger door from the inside the car. Raven's wheels started turning. "Yeah he will be riding the bench before this night is through." She unlocked her phone and shot off a quick text to her driver while she slid into the passenger's seat.

"Raven do you think I could get your undivided attention tonight?" Devon asked looking down pointedly at the phone in her hand. She counted to three and smiled locking her phone and sliding back into her Prada bag.

"Sure Devon, of course you can." Knowing 'Mr Devon' would be spending his night alone after dinner, she smiled sweetly and sat back as he pulled away from the curb and drove towards her favorite restaurant. She didn't know what the hell he thought was up but NO ONE told Raven Hicks what to do, her parents were in Denton, Texas and she was a grown ass woman. He sensed her getting upset so he reached over and lightly stroked her hand.

"I'm sorry Rave, I'm just really glad to be spending this evening with you, I didn't mean to snap at you."

"Too late for sorry." She thought to herself as she smiled even sweeter, her dimples making a cameo. "No worries Devon we're good." She watched the scenery moving by her window, loving the feel of warm air moving around in the car.

"So, how's work?" Devon asked like he was really curious, she knew better he didn't even know what she did for a living.

"It's fine. Devon how is business for you?" Knowing that's what subject he wanted to discuss anyway. He owned a very successful computer programming firm and always reminded Raven just how rich and successful he was when they spoke.

"We just obtained 30 new patents for new apps so business is good, really good." He spent the remainder of the ride to the restaurant on his favorite subject, himself.

When they pulled into the parking lot instead of the valet tent Raven had to bite the inside of her cheek to keep from snapping on Devon. Cheap ass! Just spent the last 40 minutes talking about how much money he made this last quarter but wouldn't spend ten dollars on valet?! Raven was pissed! She had to walk across this raggedy parking lot in her Manolo's! If they get so much as a scratch Devon would have hell to pay!

"Is everything okay Baby?" He asked smiling at the passenger side window. Her eyebrow shot up again.

"Baby?! Um no, you know my name. Use it." She snapped and climbed out of the car completely unassisted, no hand offered at all. She saw his jaw jump again and smiled.

"Raven, sometimes your mouth...." He trailed off as he closed her door and held her elbow as they walked towards the entrance.

Raven reached in her bag and as her hand closed around her phone, the vibration meant work not personal, her office was trying to reach her. Devon's hand grabbed hers inside her bag. She stopped walking at the door. "Devon have you lost your damn mind?!" She hissed at him glaring at his hand covering hers. Her eyes narrowed throwing fire and ice.

"Raven the least you can do is honor my request and stay off your phone damn!" He flung her hand away.

She shook her head smiling and dialed her driver. "Maurice never mind the hour, come now please." Devon's mouth flew open with disbelief

"An hour? now? Seriously Raven?!" She smiled and sidestepped Devon and entered the restaurant.

"May I help you ma'am?" The hostess asked Raven. Devon stormed in behind her his face bright red with anger.

"Yes, my name is Raven Hicks, I believe my driver called in a 'to go' order for me it was to be prepared when I arrived?" Devon stood behind her sputtering. The hostess noticed and quickly looked away.

"Why yes Miss Hicks, I will send word to have your meal prepared now, it will be up in a few minutes please feel free to have a seat." She rushed after a last uncomfortable glance in Devon's direction.

Raven sat down in one of the plush chairs and smiled sweetly at the hostess. "Thank you so much and I appreciate your time." She watched the hostess walk towards the kitchen and pulled out her phone.

Devon flopped down in the chair next to her, his anger was radiating off of him in waves. "You are so fucked up Rave, one selfish bitch." He spat. Raven looked up from her phone, she was busy deleting Devon, two in one night, impressive.....

"You still here?" She sighed. "Selfish Devon? Never that. Just resourceful enough to know when my times being wasted." She stood as the hostess returned with her meal. She grabbed the bag and walked to the door her purse on her shoulder, her jacket draped over her arm. "Oh, this is on him, thanks for dinner Devon, I'm sure it will be wonderful."

Raven winked and exited the restaurant and walked straight into the back of her town car, her driver Maurice holding the door open. "Thank you, Maurice, perfect timing as usual." She watched out the rear window in amusement as Devon stormed out of *the restaurant as the car rounded the corner heading for home.*

Chapter 1

He walked in front of her in the cafe, his cologne assaulted her senses. "Dolce and Gabbana Light Blue." She mumbled, making note that her favorite cologne smelled incredible on him. Her eyes traveled down from his caramel brown angular face to his full lips, down his muscular chest, noting that even his calves and thighs had definition and tone. He turned, Smokey grey green eyes met her blue green. His full lips spread into a heart stopping smile. "Hi." His voice sent chills through her body. She blinked several times trying to get her mouth to form words. When she remained silent, he reached for her or so she thought. Her icy glare had him chuckling. "Relax, I'm reaching for the creamer. You're in the way."   She blushed and moved so he could fix the coffee he just bought to his liking, his back to her. She stood her eyes taking all of him in again, the way his shirt stretched across his back and how he fit into his jeans had her mouthwatering. He turned sipping his coffee and looked down at her, smiling. He was at least 6'4", she loved tall men. "Umm is your name Raven?" Surprise finally snapped her out of her fog.

"Yes, it is, do I know you?" She snapped embarrassed that not only was she staring at this man like a lovesick puppy but that he knew her as well. Again, he smiled, her knees went weak in spite of her embarrassment and irritation.

"No, it's just that the server has been calling your name for the past few minutes and since we are the only two here at the moment he was either talking to you or me and my name isn't Raven, so I assumed yours was."

She blushed again and rushed forward to grab her coffee and breakfast sandwich. "Sorry about that." She mumbled and threw an extra five-dollar tip in the jar near the register. She turned to see him still there watching her smiling. She pushed past him and out the door, his baritone

"Bye Raven." wreaking havoc on her senses.

Later the same day, she was still in a snit about her actions. Her office door had been closed all day, and everyone knew that meant to leave her alone. Never in her life had she reacted to anyone like that and never would she again. What the hell was wrong with her? "Must be a lack of sex." She whispered biting her bottom lip in thought. She tried to shake those sexy ass eyes from her memory bank and made a mental note to visit the 'toy' store that weekend. She had never even considered artificial stimulation but between the way she reacted today and the way she was dropping men it was time to.

******

"Are you following me or something?" She was standing in front of a wall of vibrators, all promising 1001 ways to bring a female to orgasm. She had just picked up a 'rabbit' with lights and spinning beads, two rabbit ears vibrated when she pushed a glowing button. That teasing baritone had her blushing and cursing under her breath, of all the damn places to run into him again, he was the main reason she was here in the first damn place!

She had seen him every day that week at Cafe Jax, why should she have to change her routine? She had been frequenting the place for years. The fact that she had been there more this week than she had in the last six months meant nothing she stubbornly told herself, it was because she really did love their green tea and egg white croissants not because of him. Every day he would smile that damn smile, hold up his hands in surrender telling her he wasn't reaching for her but for the creamer even when she stood right next to the counter across the room from it. As she walked out he called out.

"Bye Raven, nice talking to you." She never said a word to him, her blush said enough.

She looked over her shoulder throwing him a dirty look, taking in the apron and nametag which read 'Kendrick' it was safe to assume he worked there. She pressed the button again and placed the now quiet and still toy back on its displays. "Do I know you?" She snapped, her eyes throwing icy sparks even though seeing him and having him this close to her again after running through her mind all day all week had chills going up her spine. She took a step to move around him and out of the store when he grabbed the same toy she had been examining.

"This is one of our best sellers, dual motors, waterproof, 10 speeds, were you looking for something new or an upgrade?" She cleared her throat and glared at him.

"'Actually, I'm looking for something for a friend, she's getting married it's for her bachelorette party." He looks down at her with a smirk, like he knew she was lying.

"Roger that. Anyway, if you have any questions or need me to show you something for your 'friend' let me know." He winked, put the toy back and left her standing dumbfounded. As much as she wanted to storm out and never look back she wouldn't give him the satisfaction. She slowly walked around the store making note of his whereabouts every time she stopped in front of a display. Each time she did he was watching her, smiling. Doesn't he have quota or commission to make? She thought to herself angrily.

        With the help of a female clerk Raven was finally able a few selections in spite of him watching her and followed her to pay for her items. Just as the clerk signed into the register he stepped up. "I got this one Toni, I will make sure you get the commission for it." Toni smiled and sidestepped to allow him access to the register.

"Thanks Kenny." She waved and went back to the sales floor. "Looks like some good choices. Your 'friend' will be very happy." Raven parked her hand on her hip annoyed.

"Don't you have anything better to do than harass me? I mean isn't this your job? Don't you work here?! Where's your supervisor? Maybe they need to know how you spend your time on the clock and let's be honest you and me come from completely different worlds and social classes so why do you continue to bother me?" She smirked, one eyebrow raised. Kendrick quietly put batteries in each item to ensure they worked then scanned and bagged them. After giving her her total and swiping her card, he handed her, her purchases and receipt.

"To answer your questions, I don't have a supervisor, I own this place and several other businesses in the area. I'm only working here tonight because the assistant manager no called/no showed and I refused to let the ladies work alone, the security guard isn't on duty until 10 and the weekend brings in all kinds of crazies. As for worlds and social class goes, I wasn't aware we were actually that different until you pointed it out, and since you did; you're right. We are in very different classes, vastly different. It appears I have class and manners and you while incredibly beautiful, does not." Raven opened her mouth to say something, but he held up his hand. "It's okay, have a good night Raven." He walked back towards the sales floor without a backward glance.

*****

"Raven you have seen preoccupied all night are you alright?" Her date asked her reaching across the table to gently take her hand. She couldn't remember his name to save her life, she just remembered it started with a 'D' and he drove a silver Jaguar XJS. She didn't need to be attracted to him for him to raise her spirits and hopefully pull her out of her blue mood. Kendrick stayed on her mind. She had tried several times to apologize to him at the cafe for her behavior at his store (Something she had never done before). After her third attempt he looked down at her with an icy glare and mumbled "Roger that." before walking out the door. In the very short time she had encountered him he had managed to shake her perfect little world to the core, she missed him, some she didn't even know and that was a very foreign feeling for her.

"I'm fine just a lot going on at work. What were you saying?"   He sighed in frustration of being ignored.

"Nothing important I guess Raven. It's still early and there is a new African American play at the Spoken Word Playhouse would you like to go?" Raven smiled at the look of irritation in his eyes, looks like another one was about to bite the dust. Matter of the fact, she was bored to tears and just wanted to go home and give her rabbit some tlc, let the images of Kendrick dancing in her head take her over the edge a few times.   She opened her mouth to decline when a certain scent began to play with her nose. She sat up straight in her chair quickly looking around the darkened dining room.

She watched him escort his date to their table, she sat back hard in her chair and drained her glass. "Oh, hell no!" She thought to herself angrily. The unfamiliar burn of jealousy began to wrap itself around her so tightly she could barely breathe. "What time does the show start?" She heard herself ask sweetly.

D-Something perked up instantly, pulled out his phone, pushed a few buttons before putting it away again. He then poured more wine in her glass. "We still have time for another glass of wine."   After putting the bottle down, he signaled for the waiter, handed him his platinum American Express card with a flourish to settle the check and sat back, taking a leisurely drink from his own glass.   "How is it a woman as beautiful as you are still single Raven?" She sighed, fighting the urge to roll her eyes at his flashing of the card and gag at his ashy hands, she hadn't noticed them until now.

       "I guess the right man just hasn't come along yet."   She stole a glance over her shoulder towards Kendrick's table, grey green eyes cut through the darkness staring back at her. He nodded in her direction and went back to speaking to his date.

Raven threw her napkin on the table in a huff. "Daryl please excuse me, I need to visit the powder room." She grabbed her Gucci clutch and stood. Her date stood as well and reached out grabbing her wrist tightly, stalling her get away.

"Darnell." She looked from his hand clutching her wrist to his face annoyed, eyebrow arched.

"What?!" She hissed embarrassed by her reaction to Kendrick as well as the scene Daryl/Darnell whatever his name was causing. Several people around them were pretending to eat but were watching them.hanging on every tense word.

"I said my name is Darnell NOT Daryl. You would think after spending all this damn money on you for dinner you would have the common decency to remember my damn name!" He ground out through clenched teeth. Raven snatched her wrist free angrily.

"And you would think your mother would have taught you to keep your hands to yourself, yet here we are both looking like fools! Do us both a favor and evaporate."   She whispered fiercely collecting her wrap as well and storming off to the lady's room, face red and burning with embarrassment.

Sitting on the pristine white couch in the lounge area of the lady's room she pulled her phone out to call her driver when the restroom door opened. She didn't bother to look up still scrolling through her phone seething with anger. "I cannot believe he had the nerve to grab me like that and here in front of him of all places!" She muttered to herself angrily.

"You good Raven?" She dropped her phone startled by the deep voice addressing her.

"What are you doing in here?! This is the LADIES room!" She exclaimed jumping to her feet. Kendrick waved her words away.

"Damn all that. Are you okay? I saw that fool grab you." He reached out gently taking her hand, running his thumb over her now bruised wrist. Her heart rate accelerated instantly, her eyes went to his, flames of desire flickered just beyond his look of concern. Goosebumps broke out all over her body, as she licked her lips nervously.

"Yes, I'm okay, now can I have my hand back so I can call my driver and get the hell out of here? Besides don't you have a date to get back to?!" She snapped trying her best to ignore how soft his hands were or what his thumb was doing to her psyche.   She had expected a look of frustration or a flair of temper on his part like most men she knew instead he just continued to gently stroke her wrist staring intently into her eyes, a small smile playing at his lips.

"So quick with that acid tongue of yours." He muttered shaking his head before slowly releasing her hand and exiting the restroom. Raven sat back down with a frustrated sigh and picked up her discarded phone from the plush carpet. After sending her driver a message of her location she dropped her phone back into her clutch and sat back, eyes closed to regroup before walking back through the dining room to exit the restaurant.

The restroom door opened again and before she had time to react she is snatched to her feet and pulled into muscular arms, strong soft lips come crashing down on her own.   It took her all of a nanosecond to realize it was Kendrick, his cologne giving him away. She placed her hands on his muscular chest with every intention of pushing him away when his hands gripped her buttocks and pulled her against his growing erection deepening their kiss, his tongue forcing its way into her mouth. Their tongues begin to dance as she gripped his shirt in tight fists, a moan escapes her as he pulls her even closer. She began to tremble all over as desire snakes up her spine, his lips moved from hers and begin to drop soft kisses on the length of her neck. Just when she all but putty in his hands he stops. His hands drop from her body as he backed away still breathing fast, now completely erect.

"Thought so. And for the record, my 'date' is actually my little sister." He snapped before storming out. Her driver's text tone fills the room as the restroom door closes loudly behind him.

****

Chapter 2

"Welcome back, it's been awhile since we saw you. Iced green tea with honey and an egg white croissant with provolone and spinach correct?" The young hostess at Cafe Jax greeted her with a smile. She had made it point to grab her breakfast elsewhere and stopped coming in over two months ago, after their encounter in the restaurant bathroom she knew it was best she stays as far away from Kendrick as she could get but a late night and a morning staff meeting had her rushing to the place closest to her office, to the place that started it all.

"Yes, and thank you so much, I really do love the service here." Raven pulled out her card to pay for her purchase when the hostess held up her hand to stop her.

" Oh no your breakfast has already been paid for, he told us to just make sure and give you this note when you came back in." The hostess handed her a light blue sealed envelope with her name written on it.

"Thank you." She mumbled absentmindedly. She placed a ten-dollar bill in the tip jar and moved down the counter to wait for her order with a frown turning the envelope over and over in her hand. She could smell the faint scent of his cologne rising from the envelope. over the scent of brewing coffee and pastries.

Hours later finally home after an exhausting 18-hour work day and scalding hot shower Raven sat cross legged on her king-sized bed, hair pulled up in a ponytail staring at the envelope from Kendrick. After deciding she was too tired to read let alone comprehend a letter from the man who had her new toys working overtime she placed the letter on her bedside table and clicked off her lamp. Just as her head hit the pillow and her eyes closed her phone rang, the special vibration let her know there was an emergency. She pressed talk while throwing back the covers 'I'm on my way." Was all she said as she redressed and rushed out the door.

****

"Dr Hicks?" Raven was called back from her thoughts, she'd been anxiously pacing waiting on the test results she ordered the minute she arrived in the E.R.

"Yes? Are the results in?" She asked hopefully.

"Yes, they are, I will let them know you will be with them shortly." The nurse stated setting the laptop on her desk before slipping out of the office quietly. Raven sighed and slipped her white lab coat back on over her mint green scrubs, her white shoes held a coffee stain from earlier in the day. Gone was the makeup, designer clothes, the attitude. Her hair was still pulled back tightly in a simple ponytail, her entire demeanor softened. Raven traveled from Dallas to Louisiana and ran her practice four days a week, procedures and surgery often scheduled on the fifth day. Her practice was #1 in Pediatric Oncology, her patients were her life. She had sacrificed everything to get where she was in her career, especially her love life. Raven decided to date on her terms and that is why she'd been trying to convince herself she had no time for someone like Kendrick. After minimal conversation and one mind melting kiss she knew he was the first man she ever really wanted to get to know, wanted to spend more than a few hours with and that scared the hell out of her. She had to maintain control and be in control at all times.

Raven logged into Jessica Monroe's chart and fought back the tears stinging the back of her eyes. She had been in remission for 4 years, but her cancer had returned. As she walked into the exam room Jessica smiled from the hospital bed and stretched her arms towards Raven for a hug. . Her beautiful face shining, her hair tied in two ponytails with floral ribbons.

"Hello Dr Rave, you look so pretty today." Jessica said as Raven sat next to her on the bed smiling.

"Not as pretty as you do beautiful girl." Mr. and Mrs. Monroe sat close by smiling strained smiles at their only child she could see the anxiety in both their faces.   This is never easy.....

*****

Chapter 3

Raven, I have tried at least a thousand times to talk myself out of this. To be honest you are everything and I do mean everything I have always hated in a woman. While you are breathtakingly beautiful you are self-centered, arrogant and quite rude and still I can't get you off of my mind. I can just imagine that one eyebrow lifted smirk moving across your face as you read this! I came to Cafe Jax for two weeks at various different times and have learned their menu by heart looking for you. When you didn't show up I was like "Good now you know it's not meant to be, move on." Yet that kiss we shared keeps reminding me that's not possible, I don't know what this is exactly I just know you feel it too. I'm not sure you will ever even get this letter being the stubborn type of woman you are but if you do, hit me up so we can figure this thing out.

Kendrick

Raven flung the letter across her bed with a frustrated scream. She didn't know what she expected but she didn't expect what she had just read. "Hit me up?!" Who the hell does he think he is that he can insult her then summon her like that?! Ugh! "I have no time for this kind of foolishness." She thought to herself as she quietly tucked the letter in the blue envelope and slid it in the drawer of her bedside table.

*****

Raven sat in the hospital cafeteria chugging down what they claimed was coffee while watching various hospital staff cliqued up while enjoying their breaks. Another six months, 3 weeks and four days had passed since she received Kendrick's letter, sadly enough she had counted. She read that letter every night in spite of herself, hadn't been on a date since then, there was no use all the men she knew bored her to tears.

"Raven Hicks, MD what brings you down here with us peasants? Slumming?" She slowly finished her coffee while considering her response. Dr Jeffrey Milton stood in front of her looking like a living 'Ken' doll with a smug smile, there was no love lost between them in fact she couldn't stand him she tolerated him as necessary, a professional courtesy.

"No actually Dr Milton just a little coffee before surgery. You know how that can be. Oh, that's right you don't, you still have your privileges revoked, don't you? Nasty thing that sexual harassment lawsuit, hope you have learned to keep your hands to yourself." She cut him deep with her words and an icy glare, she chuckled to herself as she heard him mumble fiercely

"Bitch."

****

As she scrubbed for surgery to remove Jessica Monroe's tumor the familiar scent of Dolce and Gabbana light blue reached her nose. With a frown she turned to her nurse. "Did Dr Reese change his cologne?"

She always worked with the same team, from the nurses, assistant surgeon to the anesthesiologist, Dr Morgan Reese. Her nurse Jade hung the pictures of Jessica's tumor on the illuminator shaking her head in the negative.   "Dr Reese isn't here, last minute emergency."

"Dr Hicks, this is Dr Maxwell." Her Assistant surgeon made the introductions as she entered the operating room. His grey green eyes met hers with question. She nodded in his direction and directed her attention to her sleeping patient.

"Is she ready to begin?"

After checking on Jessica and updating her parents that all of the malignant tumor had been removed, Raven took a shower and rushed towards the doctor's lounge to grab her purse and briefcase to head for home with a million questions running through her head. Their eyes met the minute she crossed the threshold.

"You're a doctor?!" They both asked at the same time.   Laughing, Kendrick sat on the old beat up couch, Raven sat in the creaky rolling chair across from it.

"You go first Raven, three questions, three answers fair enough?"

Raven sat back and closed her eyes for a moment pinching the bridge of her nose to alleviate some of tension she felt there. Even after 9 hours of surgery and as tired as she felt being this close to Kendrick had her head spinning.

"Fair enough. So, I'm a bit confused. You told me you owned businesses in the area, then here you are Dr Kendrick Maxwell., anesthesiologist." He sat up smiling shaking his head.

"Is there a question in that statement Raven or just an observation?" His eyes bore deeply into hers, she tried to ignore the messages they were sending and licked her lips nervously before asking

"How Kendrick? How are you being doctor with privileges here?!)

have worked here forever and never heard of you. Why did you tell me you owned the specialty 'toy' store if you really don't and why? Why the hell did you write that letter knowing good and well we are not compatible in any way, shape, or form?"   Kendrick sat quietly for a brief moment his eyes traveling up and down her seated form and cleared his throat.

"I think we should have this conversation somewhere else, when and where can you meet me?"

Raven threw her hands up in frustration. "Are you freaking kidding me Kendrick?! You said three questions, three answers what the hell is your damn problem?"   Kendrick stood pulled on his jacket he was holding and walked to the door.

"Yeah, I know what I said but I'm thinking this is NOT the place to show you exactly how compatible we actually are, so again when and where can we go to finish this conversation?" Raven shot an icy glare his direction contemplating on what her next move should be. Even if she suggested the time and place HE would be in control, this whole damn situation had been on his terms so far and somehow, she had to turn the tables on his grey-green eyed ass once and for all let him know SHE ran things!

"Home Doctor Maxwell. I will be heading home now, I have no more time for this conversation or you." She snapped walking over to her locker and quickly grabbing her things to leave.

"Shit! Woman why are you so damn difficult?!" He whispered fiercely, storming over to her. She turned to tell him to never ever refer to her as 'woman' as long as he was black and breathing when she was pressed up against the lockers his tongue in her mouth before she could utter the first syllable. She tried to move her head and push him away when one of his soft yet strong hands took ahold of both of her hands pinning them above her head. With his free hand he gently stilled her head and deepened their kiss when she began to kiss him back he slowly and lightly ran his fingers down her neck, to her collarbone making his way to her breast. Her nipples were already hard when he began to massage one over her silk blouse, she wore no bra just a camisole underneath. She arched against his hand moaning into his mouth. His tongue dove deeper just as his hand untucked her blouse from her pencil skirt and softly dragged his fingertips across her stomach, chill bumps broke out all over her body at the contact, a shiver ran up her spine.   He broke off their kiss breathing hard, eyes dark with desire as he looked down at her, breath coming out in pants. His hand traveled further up her blouse when his palm came in contact with her bare nipple her knees went weak. He began a slow deliberate massage as his hips ground into her his erection moving against her pubic bone. She tried to hold his gaze but her eyes fluttered closed as she moaned again. His grip on her hands laxed as he grabbed the old rolling chair and settled into it. Kendrick gently lead her until she was standing in front of him.

He leaned down and caressed her ankles, then her calves before moving her skirt up until it was up over her hips exposing her lace underwear. He gripped her buttocks and pulled her forward until she was straddling him. He kissed her neck while unbuttoning her blouse, he kissed the top of each breast in turn before pulling one breast free and running his tongue around the nipple. Raven arched her back and moved her hips grinding against his erection. The scent of her arousal perfumed the air around them. Kendrick moved to undo his pants when the doorknob of the locked door rattled.

It was like a light switch to Raven's common sense. She looked around blinking as if waking from a dream. She sprang out of his lap and pulled her skirt down then tried to button her shirt with shaking hands. She was blushing from head to toe. Kendrick remained seated, his erection still straining against his black slacks watching her with amusement dancing in his eyes, a smile tugging at the corner of his mouth.

"Do you want to open the door or should I?"

Chapter 4

Raven stood staring out of her office window, once again admonishing herself for her behavior with Kendrick in the doctor's lounge. Her face grew warm, chills of desire moved through her body and settled between her legs as she remembered his soft lips and hands touching her.   A soft moan escaped her lips as she closed her eyes and rested her head against the cool window pane.

"Dr Hicks? Are you okay?" She her eyes sprang open and she folded her arms to hide her erect nipples and cleared her throat.

"Yes- um yes I'm fine is Elias and his parents here to discuss his treatment plan?" Her nurse looked down at her feet for a moment before looking over at Raven again.

"No, they decided to forgo treatment, said God will heal him. His mother just phoned in, I advised her of the late cancellation fee." Raven sighed at length and sat down hard in her chair. She believed in a higher power and knew without Him she would have lost her mind years ago but she hated to hear when a child or anyone in fact was being denied medical treatment because of religious beliefs.

"Well hell. God willing, they will change their mind before it's too late. What's next?" Her nurse checked her tablet and smiled at her.

"Nothing. Elias was the last patient of the day. You look tired Dr Hicks, why don't you go home and get some rest while you can." Raven stood and pulled off her lab coat nodding.

"That is exactly what I think I will do. Oh, and Hannah waive the fee, they have enough to contend with." Her practice had a strict cancellation policy, she felt no call no shows and late cancellations could cost lives why this family was different she had no idea.   Hannah nodded with a frown and made a note in the chart to waive the fees.

"Ok Dr Hicks will do, and if it's okay with you after that I'm closing up and forwarding the phones." Raven grabbed her purse and briefcase and headed for the door.

"That's fine Hannah, have a good weekend."   She smiled back at her nurse and made her way to her car.

Raven settled into the driver's seat when a car's lights flashed when its alarm was disengaged. "Raven hold up!" Kendrick jogged across the parking lot to her car. Raven rolled her eyes heavenward and let out a frustrated breath.

"Yes Dr. Maxwell?" She asked through the tinted window. Although her tint was very dark he glared directly in her eyes.

"Roll the window down please Raven." She glared back starting her car and putting it in reverse.

"Leave me alone Kendrick," She snapped backing up and around him exiting the parking garage heading for home.

****

"Raven, you can't keep avoiding me forever we need to talk." Kendrick said pulling up behind her in her driveway, she had just pushed the remote to open the garage door. Raven stepped out of her car, flames of anger engulfing her.

"Have you lost your ever-loving mind?! Am I not speaking English or something?! LEAVE ME ALONE KENDRICK!" She snapped pulling out her phone, storming towards her house. Kendrick caught up with her in a few steps and reached over her shoulder and grabbed her phone from her grasp, sliding it into his back pocket.

"Raven, give me ten minutes." She glared at him before sighing in defeat and turning to enter her house.

"Fine. I am telling you right now you touch me and I am screaming like a banshee."

Kendrick followed her inside and watched in amusement as she slipped off her shoes in her mudroom and slid on a pair of worn cartoon themed slipper. "Cute shoes." She looked down and wiggled her toes loving how the slippers felt on her tired feet.

"I wear heels every day, sometimes twelve hours at a time, these are a necessity. Oh, and take off your shoes before you enter my house, I have snow white carpet and want to keep it that way." She left him in the mudroom struggling with his shoes while she went to her kitchen. "Nine minutes left Dr Maxwell," She called out pulling out the ingredients she needed to prepare a quick dinner for one. He settled into a stool facing her across the island where she had pulled out a cutting board and knife to cut the vegetables she was going to prepare.

"You cook?" He asked in surprise then smirked.

"Eight minutes and I want my damn phone back." She stated ignoring his question. Yes, she cooked she was a damn good cook not many men knew that about her they weren't around long enough to find out.   He shook his head reaching out stealing a piece of the red pepper from the cutting board.

"I will give it back in eight no make that seven and a half minutes." He popped the pepper into his mouth chewing slowly watching her. She felt the hairs on her neck stand on end watching his mouth, those sexy ass full lips had her mind on having him for dinner.

Screw a grilled chicken breast and southwestern vegetables!   "Kendrick, please just say what you have to say so I can enjoy my rare evening off." She said lying the knife to the side of the cutting board.

"Raven, why haven't you returned any of my calls or texts?"   He asked leaning forward all playfulness gone. Raven shrugged looking indifferent.

"Didn't want to."   Kendrick grabbed another slice of pepper, flipping it around before popping it in his mouth, considering her answer while he chewed.

"Interesting. The last time we 'talked' you were seconds away from riding me like your own personal hobby horse and now you have nothing to say to me."   Raven's face grew warm as she blushed memories of the two of them in the doctor's lounge came flooding back.

"That's right I had a temporary loss of my senses, now I am thinking straight and the one thing I do know is that you and I no matter how much we seem to lust for one another have no business being together. We are colleagues and as such we have a level of professionalism we should maintain at all times." Kendrick sat back chuckling folding his arms.

"We are two grown individuals and the only thing we should be maintaining is the noise level so your neighbors don't call the police." Raven reached over and pressed the button that ignited the tiny grilling surface on the island.

"Time's up Dr Maxwell please leave my phone on the table on your way out." Her Icy glare came easy as she watched him stand place her phone on the table, she silently told her hormones to 'shut up' as parts of her anatomy called out for him to stay.

"You know Raven it's too bad you never really listen unless you're the one doing the talking." His eyes met hers as he turned back around to face her.

"What do you mean?" She asked grabbing tongs to put her chicken on the grill He moved around the island until he was face to face with her.

"I asked you to give me ten minutes but not once did you ask how many minutes I planned on giving you." He turned off the grill with a flick of his wrist. "Dinner will have to wait." He whispered seductively before bringing his lips to hers. She didn't bother to try to push him away this time, her hands always ended up balled up in his shirt pulling him closer. She gripped her pants tightly while trying to convince herself that his kisses had no effect on her whatsoever. Kendrick grabbed her ass and pulled her close against his muscular body in spite of her indifference and stiff posture. When his tongue pushed its way into her mouth she threw her arms around his neck and began to kiss him back. Cupping his head in her hand she forced her tongue into his mouth with a moan. He scooped her up in his arms still kissing her and laid her down on the couch. He unbuttoned his shirt pulling it off quickly and tossing it to floor. Before she had a moment to react he had her out of her own shirt as well as her skirt and is leaned over her reclining body to kiss her again. Raven had already begun to tingle all over when his hand moved between her legs and began to massage her over her lace thong. She moaned and sank deeper into the couch moving her legs apart. He followed her still kissing her, his mouth moving from her lips to her ears, to her neck and back again. He is semi-reclining over her body knee propped between her legs.   He moved his finger past her underwear and slowly pushed it into her wet warm center and began to move it in and out. Raven arched her back to meet his finger and he suddenly stops kissing her. His smoky grey green eyes are dark with desire, staring intently into hers hand still moving in and out of her middle.

"Raven, I need to know are you 100% ready for this? Once you give me the green light I'm not stopping for shit do you understand what I'm saying? If you don't want to do this cool tell me now do you want this? Do you want me Raven?"   Raven reached down to still his moving hand she was on the brink of sexual insanity, she needed a minute to think clearly.   Once she was able to breathe normally she asked.

"What if I say 'no' I'm not ready? Is that it? Are you and I finished? Will you walk away and leave me alone?" He sighed in defeat sitting back at her feet on the couch no longer leaning over her. His erection pressing painfully against his slacks begging to be freed, he ran his hand down his face, her sexy smell lingered long after his hand left his face.

"Raven, if that's what you want then yes, I will walk out right now and leave you alone. We will see each other in passing, work together and maintain professionals above all else."

The crystal clock on her mantle second hand ticked in an otherwise silent room as they stared at each other. Eyes doing all the talking. This was it, whatever was said, whatever she decided to do she was finally in control with Kendrick.

Raven sat up and cleared her throat before licking her lips nervously. Closing her eyes and moaning his taste still there. "Kendrick I'm sorry I didn't plan on this, I'm not even sure I can do this ....I mean I only thawed out one chicken breast."

Her eyes danced with mischief as she saw his face read disappoint then confusion and finally relief. "Well I guess it's a good thing I didn't come here to eat chicken."   In one quick fluid motion he pulled her legs towards him until she was flat on her back spread her legs and buried his head between them.   He immediately began to lick her and suck her clit over her underwear. The moist warmness of his tongue and friction of the lace had her seeing stars in seconds. She felt his teeth take hold of her thong and pull softly at first then forcefully until she was fully exposed, thong torn.   His ran his tongue from her clit to her opening being sure to lap up every drop of her wetness over and over again. Raven gripped the couch, her hips grinded against his mouth. He locked his arms around her thighs and flipped her so he was now on his back on the couch and she sitting directly on his tongue. He drove his tongue deep darting in and out of her, leaving her no choice but to grind against his mouth he still had her thighs spread wide locked in his arms. She gripped the couch and road his tongue like she longed to ride his erection. She rolled her hips slowly, grinding against his mouth. He re-adjusted his head to give her clit some much needed attention, by the time he was alternating between sucking and swirling his tongue she had come twice.

"Kendrick damn!" She threw her head back, body bathed in sweat, cumming for the third time.

Kendrick lifted her off his face and sat up, he brought his mouth to hers as the aftershocks still rocked her body.

Just as she regained some semblance of normal breathing he positioned her over his throbbing erection and gripped her hips. His pants and underwear around his ankles.   "You're in control Raven, do what you feel, just don't forget at some point that control will come full circle back to me."   She shot him a wicked grin and slid down is erection giving him the ride of his life.

*****

    Raven was naked straddling Kendrick's back. In the middle of her king-sized bed. He was lying on his stomach eyes closed as she rubbed him down with warm shea butter.   After an evening of marathon sex all over her living room it was decided they should at least try to get some sleep. A steamy shower led to more sex and a bet that had the loser giving a massage.

"Mmm Raven this feels so good, make sure to get my thighs and calves I think I pulled a muscle when I lifted you against the wall in the shower." Kendrick had licked her five ways from Sunday in that shower, his finale had been to lifting her on his shoulders and pinning her to the wall while he ate her out.   Raven was still recovering from that one. She gave a feigned irritated sigh and moved down his body rubbing the back of his thighs then calves with shea butter.

"You do realize it's almost 3AM Dr Maxwell. We have to sleep at some point." Kendrick turned on his back and took her by the hand guiding her until she was lying on top of him.   He kissed her hand then her wrist going up her arm to her neck. After kissing her softly there he kept dropping feathery kisses until his lips met hers.

"You are worth never sleeping again for Dr Hicks."   She smiled down at him and softly touched his face.

"You don't know that Kendrick, as a matter of fact other than how I taste and how my body feels you don't know anything at all."   Kendrick softly kissed her hand again and looked deeply into her eyes.

"Not yet." Raven laid her head on his chest and closed her eyes. Knowing her track record with men, she thought to herself,

"Maybe not ever." As she allowed this alien euphoric feeling of contentment lull her to sleep.

Chapter 5

Raven tried to hide her smile behind the glass of iced tea she was sipping. She had just spotted Kendrick crossing the street walking swiftly to meet her for lunch at Cafe Jax.   Since the night he followed her home four months ago and made sure she spent every waking minute craving him they had been inseparable, spending all of the free time their busy schedules would allow with each other. He made her heart and body soar but she still knew she needed to maintain a semblance of control and balance when it came to him or any other man for that matter.

"Hello Beautiful."   He leaned down and kissed her softly.   Raven blushed from the top of her head to the soles of her feet. She hated pet names, when she was referred to by anything other than her name she was quick to correct the offender but when Kendrick called her 'Baby', 'Sexy', 'Beautiful' or whatever other term of endearment he called her she melted...he just didn't need to know that.

"Kendrick, I have told you time and time again, I hate it when you don't use my name. Men use pet names as a way to keep from mixing up their females." Kendrick shook his head in amusement he saw the twinkle of happiness in her eyes, the blush of contentment on her face knew she was once again fighting for control, to not allow herself to swept up in the feelings of them.

"Whatever you say Dr Hicks. I will try to remember that but just so you know your moody ass and the hospital and my businesses are more than enough to keep me occupied, happily occupied in your case." She glared over at him, attempting to look annoyed but when his eyes met hers whatever biting or smart-ass comment left. Ugh!!! This was so not her! All blush and goo goo eyed she needed to check herself this was ridiculous.

"I am not moody Dr Maxwell, I simply speak my mind. Most men are not used to that." Kendrick reached over and picked up her glass and took a huge drink of her iced tea staring at her thoughtfully.

"Rave, this is the first full day in about a month we get to spend together and I really don't want to spend it verbal sparring with you. Now Dr.

Raven Hicks, I thought we could go over to the Japanese Gardens on 8th." Raven smiled in surprise, stirring the last bit of tea in her glass.

"I love that place, although I haven't been in a while." Kendrick stood, put a tip on the table and extended his hand to Raven.

"Then it's time we remedy that." They left Cafe Jax hand in hand giggling and smiling into the early spring sunshine.

"Kendrick we aren't supposed to be over here." Raven whispered trying to pull her hand from Kendrick's. They were at the Japanese Gardens, the cherry blossoms were in bloom, a gentle breeze rained delicate pink petals on them as they walked the beautiful bridges and trails. Now Kendrick was leading her down a quiet path with fountains everywhere as well as restricted signs.

"Rave calm down and look around us beautiful isn't it?" Raven looked around for a moment, listening to the birds call and the fountains bubbling softly, she noticed koi fish swimming in the biggest fountain in the center of the path which forked with arrows and signs.

"Kendrick you are going to get us kicked out of here!" She whispered and turned to move back the way they came, she took two long strides and Kendrick pulled her close and removed petals from her hair and leaned down cupping her chin and brought his lips to hers.

"Relax Rave and trust me." She allowed her eyes to flutter closed as his lips softly skated over hers. She moved closer to him and he pulled her into his embrace, forgetting about where they were for a moment Raven deepen their kiss and pulled him even closer. Someone behind them coughed and cleared their throat loudly. They sprang apart and were staring into of eyes of two beautiful women in a white kimono with red sashes. Raven moved forward to explain why they were off the marked path when Kendrick bowed to the women and began speaking to them in what Raven could only assume was fluent Japanese. Her eyes bounced between them in surprised, her mouth opening and closing like a fish gulping for air. The women smiled at her and motioned them forward with one word "Come." Kendrick fell into step behind them, Raven was stock still unable to move. When he noticed she wasn't following them he took her by the hand and guided her up the path swiftly to catch up with the women. Questions were tripping over each other in Raven's mind but she couldn't get her mouth to work so she allowed herself to be quietly led to god knows where in the restricted area of the Japanese Gardens by Kendrick.

The women stopped in front of a small house with three steps made of bamboo and rice paper walls. The door slid open and another Japanese woman stepped out, this one much older than the other two but definitely related. Kendrick bows again but this time he spoke English. "Grandmother, this is Raven. Raven this is my Grandmother Michiko, the other two ladies are my cousins Hisa and Nami."   Raven looked at Kendrick in surprise who mouthed the word 'Bow'.   She immediately complies and Kendrick and his grandmother begin to converse in Japanese, then his cousins join the conversation. After several minutes Kendrick bowed again to his grandmother and turned to Raven. "I wanted you to meet my family, I wanted them to meet you, the woman I love. Today they want to perform a tea ceremony for us will you let them?" Raven looked from him to the three all strikingly beautiful woman smiling at her shyly.

"I have no idea what to say right now other than what is a tea ceremony?" Kendrick smiles over at his cousins.

"If you are willing to allow them to do this they will explain everything to you while you are getting ready." Raven nodded head still spinning from the fact that Kendrick said he loved her and watched as he moved further down the path leaving her in the care of his family.

A short time later dressed in a silk kimono Raven is led through another maze of paths and led to a much larger building made of rice paper walls and bamboo. She is instructed to take off her shoes and wait for Kendrick in a room simply decorated with a little more than a bench and flowers, a scroll depicting the arrival of spring. Kendrick entered from a different door wearing a gray kimono that reminded her of storm clouds. He sat down on the bench and gestured for her to join him. "You look so beautiful Raven, thank you for doing this for them and for me."   She looked down at the light blue hand painted silk running her hand down the garment softly.

"It's not me Kendrick, anyone would look beautiful in this but thank you."   He smiled over at her taking in her upswept hair and lightly applied makeup. The cousins washed away her makeup and left her with a softer more natural look.

"No trust me on this one it's all you, you are beautiful everyday but like this you are breathtaking." She felt shy and exposed for the first time in a very long time. A shiver of bad memories snaked up her spine. When she was dressed in her designer clothes and top of the line makeup she could mask any emotion she was feeling. Dressed like this in a virtually empty room she didn't know how to feel. "Did my cousins explain any of this to you?" She looked down at her manicured toes and nodded.

"Somewhat. They said your grandmother will be serving us tea." He chucked shaking his head.

"Of course, they did, there is so much more to it. It's considered an honor for them to this for you, Raven I have never brought anyone to meet my family or even invited them here. They asked to meet you even before we became a couple. I didn't realize how much I talked about you until my grandmother asked to meet this Raven, the one who stole her grandson's heart without his permission." Raven looked over at him confused.

"Kendrick how-" Her words were interrupted by a gong, they were being called to the tea ceremony.

******

Raven stretched at leisure, her alarm interrupting her dreamless sleep. She looked over at the empty side of her bed, a rose and note lie on the satin pillowcase. After the ceremony Kendrick took her out to dinner and then home. The night of lovemaking *she had hoped for was instead a night of tense discussion and hurt feelings.*

Raven, as luck would have it, I am not now nor have I ever been like 'most men'. You kill me Rave. You spend so much of the time we have together trying to find a reason to argue, reading too much into things instead of letting go and allowing what is happening between us to happen. You have gotta know I am here with you, trying figure us out right along with you. You are a beautiful woman Raven and a very talented and skilled physician, you have a compassion and love for children that surpasses any other doctor in your area of expertise. man would love to build a life with the person you are on paper. That being said the person you show the world, the snarky, glaring bitch you try to say is the real you are just a facade, a farce to hide your insecurities and fears. I don't know either of those women nor do I want to build a anything with them. The woman I want is the real Raven. The one who snorts when she laughs when something is really funny, who sings old Motown classics loud and off key in the shower, who cries out and trembles in her sleep and only quiets when I pull her into my arms gently. The woman who drank tea from my grandmother and kissed her hands softly to thank her when the ceremony was over. Who sat for another two hours listening to my grandmother's story of forbidden love and being disowned for loving the 'wrong man', the heartache of how she lost him.

Tears ran down her face when she wept about hearing how my grandmother buried her husband, son and daughter in law, daughter and son in law who all died in a house fire in Alabama but kept going with a shattered heart because her grandchildren needed her more than grief did. Why can't I have that Raven moving from this day forward? I declared my love for you in front of my family today and you never acknowledged it. If you aren't there yet I get that but hell could you at least tell me that so I know where I stand with you? The woman whose face lit up like a Christmas tree when her eyes met mine when I walked into Cafe Jax today, that's who I want. I have no idea why you have to be so controlled all the damn time and wish you would let me in. I wish you would trust me.

Kendrick

Raven swiftly wiped the tears from her eyes as picked her clothes for the day and went to shower. Her venomous words from the night before struck like stinging frozen rain. She told Kendrick she had not wanted or asked to be loved that was all on him. Meeting his family and everything that had followed was again all on him. She refused to give her heart away until she was ready to do so no matter how much he made her legs shake. They were colleagues with benefits nothing more. His pained face would be forever burned in her memory. The part of her *that wanted to be loved, wanted forever with Kendrick begged and pleaded for her to stop tell him the real reason why she deemed herself unlovable and never let anyone get to close but instead she pushed away the only man she would ever truly love.*

Chapter 6

A much younger Raven sits quietly in the hospital cafeteria absentmindedly twirling her engagement ring on her finger while waiting on her fiancé Dr Marc Mendel to join her for lunch. When twenty minutes soon turned into an hour, Raven quickly downed a protein shake on her way back to the 3rd floor triage area.   After treating the first of five gunshot victims she would see that night at St Charles General Hospital she quickly forgot Marc's no show at lunch.

"I really don't know he sees in her skinny stuck up ass. She isn't that cute

and I bet you he only proposed to her to make his daddy happy and get his money."   Raven was standing outside the supply closet a few nights later when she heard an LPN named Clover talking about her (again).

Marc had carried on a long-term love affair with Clover until the higher ups found out and as Clover's superior he was ordered to end the relationship and was reassigned. That was a year before he met Raven. While he was thrilled to be away from Clover's loud mouth and her classless friends on a daily basis, he continued to sleep with her filling her head with lies and promises. Clover assumed their next logical steps were down the aisle until the night Marc called for an assistant when he was performing an emergency bypass surgery. The only physician available was from his old hospital, that physician was Raven Hicks. While in school for Pediatric Oncology she was hired in triage. He dropped Clover like a bad habit.

From that day in the OR he shamelessly pursued Raven and after a month her house looked like a floral shop. Having no idea of his history she began dating, then became engaged to Marc, not knowing until after he placed the ring on her finger who Marc was to the nurse who she now worked very closely with.

Raven cleared her throat, squared her shoulders back and yanked open the door. Clover and one of her 'girls' jumped in surprise and started grabbing random supplies pretending that was the reason they were in the closet.

"Oh, hey Dr Hicks was there something in here we could grab for you?" Clover asked through a plastic smile. "Raven's smile was just as plastic when she answered.

"I need some electrodes for the 12 lead in room one, there are none on the cart." Clover sighed nostrils flaring.

"Dr Hicks why would you even need those? I did that EKG half an hour ago." Raven grabbed the box off the shelf took enough to perform the test as well as extras for the cart.

"No, actually you performed the test on the patient in room three, the leg injury not the chest pain in room one. So, I was going to get it taken care of, no worries." Raven turned on heel and went to tend to her patient.

"Dr Hicks, have you seen Clover by chance? I need her." The charge nurse asked her looking frantic.

"Oh, she was just in the supply closet a minute ago." Raven answered and continued to room one. Several hours later Clover and two of her girls were shooting daggers at her each time she passed and refused to answer call lights for any of her patients. Fed up with their behavior Raven went to them to clear the air. "Look ladies, I know you don't particularly care for me or even working with me and that's fine. HOWEVER, I refuse to allow that to put a patient's well-being at risk simply because I am their doctor. I am in no mood for sophomoric high school behavior so are you going to do your job or should we send you home for the evening?" Clover slammed her pen down and advanced on Raven until they were nose to nose.

"Look you uppity bougie bitch I don't know what you thought but you have no authority to tell us to do anything or to send us anywhere. Dr Morgan is gone for the day and he was in charge NOT you and as far as your patients go look at the notes, all of their needs have been met, we just met them from here! I know it was you who snitched to the charge nurse too. Keep messing with me and see what happens. Don't let those two little letters after your name or that ring on your finger make you think you're special Dr Hicks." She snapped her fingers and with a roll of her neck she was moving back to her seat behind the nurse's stations right in front of the monitors. Someone just out of sight cleared her throat and walk over to them. It was the charge nurse from earlier.

"Rachael I-I-I thought you were at lunch." Clover stuttered and turned bright red, the nurse named Isabel to her right rushed over and grabbed the papers lying in the copier tray, the one named Naomi to the left grabbed her stethoscope off the desk muttered about re checking vitals on a patient.

"Well ladies it would seem while the cat's away the mice will play huh? Clover I thought I made myself very clear earlier about your expected performance here and yet you still take it upon yourself to undermine and blatantly ignore orders and requests of help from Dr Hicks. Isabel and Naomi, I expected so much more from you. I am disappointed in you both as well. You are all relieved of duty and suspended for a week." Rachael relieved Naomi of the papers from the tray after skimming the first page. She shook her head sadly. "Better still, your suspension will be indefinite until we can get all of this figured out, not doing your job and disrespecting one of our physicians is one thing, falsifying patient records are another. This is something we will not tolerate here."

All three women stood and began to speak at once trying to plead their case. Raven sighed shaking her head sadly and moved away from the nurse's station.   Yes, they had all brought disciplinary action on themselves, but she hated to see anyone throw their jobs and quite likely their careers away over something so trivial.   She would never understand why as women they were quick to blame the woman and leave the man blameless.

*****

"Raven what the hell happen with Clover tonight? She is blowing up my phone tripping about you getting her fired!" Marc shouted in her ear as soon as answered her phone. Raven sighed and ran her hand down her face it was 3am and she just got home.
"Marc first of all hello sorry I missed you at lunch. Second Clover and

her friends got themselves suspended by ignoring my patients' lights and falsifying patient records. She had already been reprimanded once when this happened, so that is all on Clover not me!"   Marc slammed his car door.

"She said you just walked away laughing Raven, you never said anything to de-escalate the situation. I know she is just a nurse but we are supposed to look out for our own Raven." Raven was sitting at the island in her kitchen sifting her mail and immediately saw red.

"Marc, first of all, I never said she was 'just a nurse. Second, look for who exactly? Just because we are both black does not give her a free pass to act a damn fool, and third why the hell do you even care about what is going on with that female? I thought you said she was ancient history. I mean are you fucking kidding me?! Am I supposed to take up for a silly petty female who put MY patients in danger with her negligence and even talked two other nurses into doing the same thing just because you broke her heart?! You cannot really be that stupid! If someone on your shift did even a fraction of what she did tonight you would have had her written up and off the floor so fast the ink wouldn't have had time to dry before she was escorted out."

"I get that Raven, but you know everyone already sees you as stuck up and unapproachable. how do you think it's going to look when word gets out?" Raven pulled her ponytail holder off her hair and ran her fingers through it frustrated.

"How's it is going look to who Marc? I could give a rat's ass of what those small-minded petty people you are referring to think of me. I did not graduate top of my class early mind you to keep up appearances. Unlike Clover, I was doing my job. Asking her to do hers shouldn't have been seen as the issue she made it out to be." Marc sighed.

"Yeah I know. I just feel bad for her you know?" Raven rolled her eyes heavenward then sat up straight as realization hit her.

"Marc, why do you know or even care about what she's going through? You're still sleeping with her, aren't you?"   Muffled swearing could be heard on his end of the connection.

"Raven how can you even ask me something like that? I am in love with you, I want to marry you please don't get insecure on me now. I can't take it. I am going to chalk all of this up to stress from school and work on your part and we can finish this conversation another time."

"No Marc. I am NOT stressed nor am I the little naive fool you take me for, there is no need to continue this conversation another time, it's over!" Raven slammed her phone cracking the screen, when it began ringing again she slid it off the counter and stormed off to take her shower as it shattered and broke on her marble tile.

Chapter 7

"Raven thank you for finally agreeing to meet with me so we could talk, I know emotions were quite high the other night and we need to clear the air." Marc sat back after pouring her a glass of white wine as she walked up and settled in the chair across the table from his. Raven was still ticked off at him for blaming her for Clover's termination not to mention she was all but sure she was right that he was still sleeping with her. Her engagement ring was in the ring box it came in in her purse, regardless of what he said she would be returning it tonight, she was no one's fool.

"Marc, I said all I needed to say the other night, it's over. I refuse to be with let alone marry a man who could actually put the feelings of his supposed ex-girlfriend above mine." Marc waved her words away like they were nothing.

"Clover was never my girlfriend, she was a woman whose company I enjoyed from time to time BEFORE we met. I could not take her seriously. She is just a nurse and is content to be just a nurse for the rest of her life. The woman I need by my side is you. You are flawless in every way. You are beautiful, well spoken, intelligent, goal oriented and you know when to take a step back and allow your man to lead." Raven picked up the glass of wine and for a split second considered tossing it in Marc's arrogant face. Yet she was not one to cause a scene so instead she took a small sip before speaking and smiled sweetly.

"Clover may not be one of my favorite people but she is not JUST a nurse. Nurses are the backbones of every aspect of our jobs, we as physicians might take the time to realize that we are only as good as the nurses we work with and I am humble enough to realize that. I am a better doctor because of them and all they do for us. I want to thank you Marc for finally showing your true colors and the disgusting pig you are BEFORE I made the terrible mistake of marrying you or I shudder to think starting a family with you-" An envelope dropped in middle of the table knocking over one of the water glasses, disturbing the plates and silverware.

"Bitch you know good and damn well you can't have no kids; his or anyone's." Clover scoffed and pulled her too tight dress over her hips, she looked like she was either drunk or hungover as she flopped down in the chair between them.

"When were you going to tell him huh? Or were you going to continue to allow him to think you were all woman?" She smirked and slid the sealed envelope over to Marc.

"Clover, you need to get your loud ass up and go home. I have told you repeatedly it's over." Marc whispered fiercely between clenched teeth. His jaw flexed angrily.

Tears sprang up in Clover's eyes instantly. "See how you are? I gave up everything for you, gave you all of me and you chose her, this phony, stuck up bitch of a he/she! I would have given you everything you asked for Marc. A wife, a home, a family something she will NEVER be able to do isn't that right 'Dr. Hicks?'" She smirked grabbing Raven's wine glass and draining it. "Even though you treat me like shit, like I don't matter, I still look out for you because I love you Marc." She drunkenly forced the envelope in his hand. Raven gathered her things quietly flames of embarrassment and fear of what Clover just said making her face hot as she watched the scene unfold.

"Goodbye Marc." She placed the ring box on the table, stood and turned as she heard Marc rip open the envelope.

"What the fuck?!" Marc exclaimed but she continued towards the exit of the restaurant on shaking legs both too embarrassed and afraid to turn around. Her trembling hand had closed on the lever of the dark glass exit door when she heard Clover cry out

"Marc no!" She turned too late.

"You were born a man you lying, sneaky bitch?!" Marc grabbed her by her hair and smashed her face against the door and everything went black.

Chapter 8

Raven pulled the photo album from her desk drawer and settled on the bed. She slowly turned the pages, pieces of her past she longed to forget seemed to shout out her. Pictures of her cut broken and bruised face made her ache all over as if it just happened yesterday. Marc putting her head through that glass door caused her to undergo seven different reconstructive surgeries on her broken eye socket, nose and mouth alone. All of her teeth had broken on impact along with her right jaw. She awoke from a medically induced coma a month after the incident. Her mother and father by her bedside thanking God she was alive and begging her for forgiveness for taking away her right to choose.

Her birth certificate sat on the opposite page of those pictures. 'Male' scratched out and female written in by her own hand flashed like a neon sign, a reminder of who she was and always had been. She was not a transsexual like Clover and Marc wrongfully believed and filled her voicemail accusing her of, she was intersex. She was born with both male and female sex organs, a penis and a vagina. Internally she was all female and since she was more female than male she underwent surgery to remove the penis when she was two years old and started hormone replacement therapy as soon as puberty hit. Her mother called them her vitamins and it wasn't until she came across her birth certificate years later before graduating high school that she was told the truth.   Anger cannot begin to describe what she felt for her parents at the time. The betrayal, the lies, everything about the situation had her seeing red. Once she was older she realized her parents did the best they could with the information available at the time and also that she could play a victim her whole life or continue to move forward and become all she wanted to be in life and more. She graduated summa cum laude from Harvard Medical School and made it her mission to help the sick and helpless.   She also hired the best plastic surgeons and physician's money could buy and every part of her body was sculpted and crafted to her liking, her own idea of perfection. She had just finished when she met Marc.

She flipped through more pages of the scrapbook, pictures of her progression of healing documented to present day. The same team of doctors were hired again and she spared no expense when it came to the reconstruction of her face. The date of her last surgery was five years ago and her scars were no longer visible anywhere but, in her mind, she saw them every day. Letters of hate and homophobic slurs from Marc who was now in prison for aggravated assault and attempted murder were tucked between the last page of pictures and the back cover of the album as a reminder of what happens when she let a man get too close. Now here was Kendrick with her proclamations of love and devotion had no idea who or what she was and she knew that now was the time to walk away before she caused him or herself anymore hurt or pain. She kicked herself for letting things go as far as they did; she knew better!

******

Raven scrubbed for surgery. Elias' parents had finally decided to go with medical intervention after all and seeing how much his tumor had grown, she immediately had him scheduled for surgery.   His sparkling blue eyes and infectious smile and dimples ran laps in her mind on repeat. She prayed she wasn't too late to save him.   As she walked into the OR Kendrick's eyes met hers before moving back to the monitor with Elia's heart rate and other vital signs. He nodded to advise her they could begin and she shifted her focus back to Elias.

She paced back and forth waiting on the results of his full body scan, she had attempted to get some charting done but until she knew what his results where she wouldn't be able to focus on anything else.   When someone knocked on the door she immediately checked her phone out of habit first. Her nurse knocked again before entering and quietly handed her the

EMR.   His MRI had detected more tumors, his cancer had metastasized, she was too late.   Raven passed the tablet back and sat for a moment her head in her hands as she got herself together.

"Dammit, if only they would have let me treat him when we initially found it." She mumbled through her hands, tears leaked through her hands. Her nurse rushed over placing the tablet face down on the desk.

"Dr Hicks you did everything you could to help him, you have no reason to feel like you did anything wrong!"

Raven sat up and looked over at the older nurse Cynthia who had been with her the last seven years.

"Thanks Cynthia in my heart I know that, I just wish it didn't have to come to this he's only a baby, he's three years old!"   Cynthia reached over and handed Raven her water bottles a look of concern on her face. Raven had never reacted this strongly to a child who was not going to make it, she was always saddened and upset but never had she broke down in tears ever! "I have to go tell these people their baby boy only has about 6 to 8 months to live and that's if they elect to let him have chemo."   Cynthia grabbed a washcloth and wet it handing it to Raven.

"This is the part of the job we hate, but it's part of the job nonetheless. Pull yourself together then we can break the news to them together."

With a heavy heart and feeling so tired she could barely lift her legs to take the next steps into her house Raven dragged her purse and briefcase to her room and tossed them in the chair of her vanity. A long shower and quick dinner were first on her list then she was determined to get her charting done.   Elias parent had taken the news as to be expected and after sitting with them in his room and assuring them at least a dozen time they were not being punished for not trusting God, their son had an aggressive and rare form of neuroblastoma, they agreed to allow him to have chemotherapy in the hospital for three days every three to four weeks. The treatment may not save his life but it would prolong it. After a long hot shower, she felt rejuvenated enough to get her charting done and make a quick and easy dinner before heading to bed. Her phone alerted that she had a new text message, it was from Kendrick: 'I saw Elias' father in the cafeteria, told me about his prognosis. I'm so sorry Rave, if there is anything I can do to help let me know. I miss you. If only you would talk to me you would know you are not in this alone. Take care of yourself goodnight.' Her finger hovered over the delete button, at the last minute she changed her mind and exited the message and put her phone on silent, then the charger. Tears wet the pillow beneath her head.

Chapter 9

"How is this even possible?!" Raven asked her doctor pacing back and forth.

"Raven why don't you have a seat? We can discuss it." Raven glared at him, eyes brimmed with tears once again, arms folded biting her thumb nail.

"I would rather stand so when your nurse gets back with my blood work and proves once and for all that this something other than pregnancy, I can get the hell out of here and move on with my life already!" Raven took a home pregnancy test after throwing up every meal for twelve weeks straight and breaking down into tears when the elevator doors wouldn't close when she pushed the 'closed' button. She had never been an emotional person. Being in her line of work she would never last wearing her emotions on her sleeve. In the past twelve weeks everything made her cry from love songs to puppies and now it would seem even malfunctioning elevators. Not believing the positive result she rushed over to her most trusted doctor and colleague Dr Reginald Bradley who performed a second test using her urine sample and the result was again positive. She was convinced she had developed some rare disease causing her to have a false positive and demanded the test be repeated with her blood.   Dr Bradley shook his head in amusement and sat back smiling.

"Raven I have been your doctor for the last 17 years and I assure there is no mistake, you are pregnant." Raven threw her hands up in frustration still pacing.

"How Dr Bradley how?! You told me even with all my hormone replacement therapy me getting pregnant was impossible!" She flopped down in the chair in front of his desk in frustration.

"No, I never said impossible I did say it was rare for an intersex woman to become pregnant."

She screamed into her hands trying to control her rollercoaster of emotions. "How rare?!" He reached over his desk and took her hands in his.

"It's rare Raven but not impossible. Intersex females can safely carry a baby to term in most instances just as another woman can. You were born with both reproductive organs on the outside but inside you were born and have always been female."   Dr Bradley's nurse walked in and handed him a slip of paper.   He sighed looking suddenly serious as he slid the paper across the desk to Raven, his nurse left the room. With shaking hands Raven took the paper and read the result. She looked from the paper to him in disbelief. His eyes now danced with amusement. "Yep still pregnant. Now that we've established that we should see how far along you are and figure out your due date."

Raven sat Indian style in her bed, her hands cupped over her still flat stomach. She turned the ringers up on both her house phone and cell so she would hear them ringing when they told her they made a mistake. She had wanted to believe more than anything she was truly pregnant but after all she had been through she knew not to get her hopes up. According to Dr Bradley her due date was December 4th, would he finally believe her once the date came and went and no baby? She held a grainy ultrasound picture in her hand, her name was printed on it, she had seen the flickering heartbeat, heard it whooshing and she still doubted it.   If she was pregnant, Kendrick was the father and after the way she treated him the last time they talked. How would he react?

*****

He was here, on her doorstep looking as wonderful as ever. She was planning on inviting him over for dinner to tell him about the baby. She finally allowed herself to believe she was pregnant and was convinced the child already had her attitude. As if arguing its own case, she seemed to get noticeably more ill since finding out she was indeed pregnant.   Ginger tea and ginger ale were now her go-to drink, dizzy spells now had her swooning like a 'belle' in the south in August. Before she could reach out to Kendrick he reached out to her, said he needed to see her, refused to take 'no' for an answer.

"Hi." Was all she said when she opened the door.   He looked down at her and his eyes red, had he been crying?

"Hello Raven. Thank you for seeing me on short notice. I know busy you are most days."   Little did he know she was interviewing physicians to be her partner in her practice. If these last few weeks had been any indicator of things to come in this pregnancy she was going to need to cut her hours.   She motioned him inside with a look of concern.

"No problem. Kendrick is everything okay?"   He slipped off his shoes and moved towards her couch then stopped short and stood in front of one of her matching chairs.

"May I sit?"   He asked quietly. Raven nodded and sat across from him.

"Ok Kendrick. I can see by looking at you I've answered my own question you are not okay, Kendrick what's wrong?"   He cleared his throat pinching the bridge of his nose to keep his tears at bay, it didn't work. Tears slid quietly down his face.

"My grandmother passed away." Raven's heart sank as she gasped clutching the charm on her necklace.

"Michiko?! Kendrick I'm so sorry! May I ask what happened?"   He shrugged fighting back tears.

"We don't know she went quietly in her sleep. We all had dinner as a family and she went to bed like normal, the next morning I received a frantic call from Nami just as I was prepping for surgery saying she thought she was sick. I told her to call an ambulance and I would meet them at the hospital when I was done. The attending said she died sometime in the night." My cousins found her and I dismissed them. It is my responsibility to look after them and I wasn't there when they needed me most."   He quietly stated tears wet his face and gathered at his chin before dropping at his feet. Raven stood to comfort him when a wave of nausea had her running from the room and into the half bath down the hall. After being sure she was done heaving she was brushing her teeth when he knocked on the door. "Raven, are you okay in there, I'm sorry I didn't realize you were sick when I asked to come over." Raven glared at her reflection in the mirror admonishing herself.

"You need to tell him asap!" She pointed a manicured finger to herself and opened the door after wetting a washcloth for Kendrick if he needed it. "I will be okay Kendrick and I am not the one you should be worried about right now. How are your cousins?" She asked passing him the washcloth.

He took it from her with a frown. "They are not taking it so well. I am making all of the arrangements myself. What's this for your subtle way of saying I have boogers or something?" He smiled weakly at his own joke.   She walked around him to the kitchen, stomach still upset.

"No when I cry, warm towels always seem to relax me, I thought it might help you too." She answered putting her tea kettle on the stove. Kendrick smirked a little.

"You cry? I am actually surprised you were born with tear ducts." Raven pulled a cup for her tea out of the cupboard and stared over at Kendrick, fighting the urge to rip him apart when he was already in pain.

"Now see I was going to offer you a cup of tea but with that last little comment you can drink water and give me back my damn towel sees the next time I be nice to your ass!" She tried to snatch the towel from his hands but he held it tight and after a few minutes of tug of war he yanked it so that she fell up against him, her tender breasts slammed into his solid chest. "Ouch Kendrick you play too damn much!" She complained pushing away from him. His arms locked around her pulling her close until her head was against his chest.

"I know we aren't together right now, but I need to hold you even if it's just for a minute, even if it is a lie." He whispered into her ear. She circled her arms around his waist and they rocked slowly in each other's arms. The only sound between them was the ticking of her clock and their breathing for several minutes. Her eyes were closed, drinking in the smell of him wishing they could be like this always when the shrill screech of the kettle startled them.   They looked at each other began to speak at the same time.

"Raven I-" "Kendrick I'm-" They both chuckled nervously, the kettle continued to sing.

"You go first." She told him, after her news she doubted he would even remember what he was going to say.

"Raven, I'm going to Japan. My grandmother made us promise to have her services and bury her in her homeland. I don't know when or if I'm coming back. I have hired a management company to run the stores. My colleagues will be taking over my surgery schedule indefinitely.

Raven saw red immediately and pushed out of his arms.

"Why are you here Kendrick?! Did you want one more screw for the road?! If that was your plan I am NOT your girl! You wasted a trip, hell I would have found out soon enough when you were no longer the anesthesiologist for my surgeries, would have been way easier too!" She stormed over to the kettle snatched it off the burner and splashed water into her teacup and on her hand.

"Dammit!" She rushed over and ran cold water on it immediately, unshed tears making her eyes burn, she wouldn't give him the satisfaction! Kendrick rushed over still speechless at the words she hurled at him and rewet the towel she had given him and wrapped it around her hand.

"Do you have any aloe?" He asked going into 'doctor mode' examining her hand.   She pointed to the hall closet and he came back with the tube.   He led her to the dining room table and unwrapped the towel, her hand was red but no blistering; she was lucky.   He quietly and gently spread the cream on her skin before speaking again. "Raven you have fought me, us at every turn and in true Raven form you only listen to what you want to hear." An uncomfortable pause.

"I wasn't finished. I want you to come with me to Japan. Not permanently unless that's what you decide to do, but for now it would just be a vacation.   I have no idea if I'm a

glutton for punishment or a stark raving fool but I love you Rave and I need you with me. If my grandmother's passing taught me anything, it taught me that life is too short and none of us are promised tomorrow. Raven stop fighting it, I know you love me too. Marry me."
Raven closed her eyes for a moment and spoke carefully.

"Kendrick, I have never met anyone like you, and I doubt I ever will again. As much as I wish I had the luxury of following you around the world, I do not. My work, my practice is very important to me, those children and their families depend on me. I can't let them down for anything, this is life I've chosen Kendrick. I'm sorry."

Kendrick quietly finished tending to

her hand and kissed it softly. After slipping his shoes back on and looked over at her for the longest time before whispering, "Sayonara." Softly and closing the door softly behind him.

Chapter 10

It has been said "If you want to make God laugh you tell him what you have planned." In Raven's case nothing drove that point home more than the day she scrubbed up for her last surgery before her 'Dr Bradley ordered maternity leave.' She had been instructed in order to carry this baby safely to term, she needed to take a leave of absence from work as soon as possible. That was three months ago and now hitting the 27-week mark in her pregnancy, it was time. Once Kendrick left she threw herself even deeper into her work. She was careful but worked as hard as she ever did before she was pregnant, sometimes even harder. When she was not working she thought too much about her life, her baby, but most of all about

Kendrick. Now that the conversion of the two guest rooms in her house into a nursery were complete, she had no idea what she was going to do at home all day.   She looked over at the full body scan images of Elias' sister Adrianne, she was six years old. Her tumor was isolated, the size of a quarter. With chemotherapy and radiation, she should be able to lead a pretty normal life after treatment, her parents didn't hesitate in the least to start treatment when her bloodwork came back abnormal. Her mind briefly flashed back to Elias and his infectious smile and dimples, he passed away two months ago after fighting as hard as his little body could. Raven cried for days after he passed away. Being pregnant she wasn't allowed to visit him with the treatment he was receiving at the end of his life.   She did visit his grave site at the Rosehill Children's Cemetery and placed an Aquaman action figure there. In the small time she knew him, she learned he was his favorite superhero because aquaman loved the water just like he did. His gravestone was engraved with waves and a picture depicting Elias holding hands with who she assumed was Jesus. Underneath the picture it read

"Let the seas rage on, your lifeguard walks on water."

Every surgery since Kendrick left was bittersweet. The gray-haired old man who had replaced him was always full of personality and sang old Sam Cooke songs to make her smile after *they were finished with a procedure. She would miss him and her whole team. Her patients would be cared for by the new physician in her practice Dr Mandra Mills while she was on leave. She hated having to leave them but she had to do what was best for her and her baby.   "Okay ladies and gentlemen, let's save this baby's life." She announced when she walked into the OR. She looked over to see the smiling eyes of the gray-haired anesthesiologist to give them the signal to begin. Instead gray green eyes bounced from her face to her protruding belly and back again before blinking and nodding slowly giving her the signal to begin. Shit!*

*****

Kendrick pounded on her door just before midnight of the same day. She was curled up on the couch hugging a pillow watching t.v. The text he sent simply said 'On my way," She just made it to the door when he started to pound on it again. She swung it open giving him a dirty look. "No! Don't even start with me! Raven what the hell?!" He stormed passed her then gestured to her stomach. She opened her mouth to speak, but he held up a hand to stop her. "Before you start with your snarky ass remarks and attitude all glaring and shit let me remind you, you have no right, no right to do any of it! Now explain." He still had on hospital shoe covers but was wearing a pair of jeans and button-down shirt. If this wasn't such a tense situation it would be funny. Not knowing where to begin she simply stated.

"Kendrick, I'm pregnant." He scoffed and flung himself down into a chair.

"Yeah well no shit! Mind telling me why I am just now finding out about this?" Raven sighed and ran her hand down her belly.

"Your Grandmother had just died and I was going to tell you the last night we spoke but after you started talking about honoring her wishes and going home I didn't want to be the reason you didn't follow through. I mean I wasn't even sure this was a viable pregnancy. Then you left and I tried to call you when I found out what

I was having but your number was disconnected, so I thought it was God's way of telling me to handle this on my own."   Kendrick looked at her in disbelief.

"By having my baby without me?! Do you have any idea how stupid and selfish you sound right now Raven? There is email, social media, hell snail mail you could have found me if you really tried."   She stood up and poured herself a glass of milk.

"Kendrick, I don't want to argue and you believe what you want. I did try to reach you, once I knew for sure this was a viable pregnancy I even went to the Japanese Gardens to speak to your cousins only to be told you were all in Japan, they refused to give me your forwarding address no matter

how many times I asked. As far as social media and email goes I don't have
any of the time-wasting sites people find so entertaining and my nurse manages my email both personal and business. The contact information in the hospital directory bounced back too. I did fill up a generic voicemail they had listed for you, I never knew if you got them so I just asked you to call me when you could. I called it every day until it told me the mailbox is full. I am bitch Kendrick but I'm not a fucking bitch." His face softened a little, just a little his jaw was still working.

"So how far along are you? When are you due?" She finished her milk and looked over at him.

"I am about 27 weeks along, I am due December 4th but if any problems arise it might be earlier."   He watched her hands moving on her stomach as she talked, when he saw her t-shirt jump on its own he looked up at her in surprise.

"Was that the baby?" He asked still watching her stomach move into odd shapes.

"Yeah, she is really active at night. I am used to it now, in the beginning I was like a zombie." He reached over and stopped short of touching her belly.

"Do you mind?"   He asked still watching the baby move.

"Normally yes, but she's your baby too go ahead." Kendrick kneeled in front of her and placed his hands on either side of her belly. The baby kicked at the added pressure immediately. Kendrick laughed and shook his head.

"Amazing, already acting up." Raven watched him through the tears forming in her eyes.

"Kendrick?" He looked up at her smile fading a bit.

"Yes?" She looked down her hands and took a deep breath.

"I want you to know I am sorry for everything." He moved his hand off her belly and sat back in his chair.

"It's good to hear you say that, in time I might be able to forgive you."

She sighed and stood to rinse her glass and put it in the dishwasher. She fought harder to keep from crying. She hated herself for pushing him away but even more so for hurting him so badly.

But now was not the time to cry, she would let that floodgate loose when she went to bed, like she did every night since she last seen him.

"I understand and hope you will." They stood staring at each other from across the island, he finally looked away for a moment then back at her.

"Raven, can I ask you something?" She nodded still holding the glass.

"Of course. What is it?" He paused for a moment before speaking.

"Are you and baby ok? I mean with you being how you are, I would hate for you to put either of your lives in danger." Raven's face burned hot, eyes dilated with fear.

"W-wh-what do you mean being how I am?" Marc's angry distorted face moved to the forefront of her mind. Kendrick licked his lips nervously.

"You were born intersex, right?" He asked. The glass slipped out of hand and smashed on the floor. "Good lord Raven we are going to have to ban you from going in the kitchen when we are talking I swear." Kendrick tipped over the broken glass and swept her in his arms settling her on the couch. She was in shock, staring at him disbelief. She watched as he swept up the shattered glass and placed in a paper bag before throwing it in her outside trash, when he joined her on the couch with she asked barely above a whisper.

"How long have you known?!" He reached over and touched her belly again.

"Since the first time we made love." Her mouth dropped open in surprise. He shrugged sadly.

"I told you Raven I loved you nothing you could have told me would have changed that, if only you would have trusted me enough to tell me."   Tears slowly spilled from her eyes and down her face realizing what she lost by constantly pushing Kendrick away.   He knew who she was and had loved her anyway.

"Kendrick?" He reached over and wiped her tears away.

"Raven?"

"Ever since I found out I was having a girl I knew what her name was."   He shook his head smiling.

"Typical Raven, I have no say so in naming our daughter either huh? What do you want to name her?" He asked with a teasing smirk.

"Michiko after your Grandmother, would that be okay?"   Blue green eyes met grey green hopeful and earnest. He wiped away his own lone happy tear.

"That would be perfect. Thank you Raven."

Chapter 11

Raven looked down at her daughter smiling. The baby's eyes were so much like her fathers at the moment but they changed colors almost by the minute. Her little face bunched up in a frown as her temper flared like her mother's, swiftly and without warning. Before she could pick her up, Kendrick scooped her up into his arms before she sounded off. "What is that about little woman?" He asked her smiling down at her.

"Do you mind if I feed her?" Raven asked with a perfectly sculpted eyebrow arched. Kendrick shot her a dirty look and kissed the baby on her forehead passing her to her mother.

"Michiko, your mother is such a jealous woman. What are we going to do with her?"   Raven positioned the baby to breastfeed ignoring Kendrick.

After consulting with Dr Bradley and him reiterating that Raven needed to rest as much as possible until she gave birth, Kendrick moved in. No negotiations or discussions he made it clear his job was to keep them both healthy and safe and that is what he intended to do.   He stayed in the guest room on the same floor as her room and the nursery in case she needed anything. She had just moved back into her room after spending the last 10 weeks on the main floor in her smallest guest rooms as she was ordered to avoid the stairs. Kendrick cooked, ran errands, and made sure she was healthy and comfortable, even ran out or cooked in the middle of the night when she had cravings. As she got closer to her due date he cut his hours at the hospital too. "Can't be in the middle of surgery when you go into labor." He had said when she told him he didn't have to it. When it was time, Maurice, her driver had to take them to the hospital, Kendrick was too nervous to drive and refused to leave her side. 12 hours of labor and then a c-section, (failure to progress) and they welcomed Michiko into the world. He had kissed her softly on the forehead and thanked her for having their baby but other than that not one sign of affection other than common courtesy. It was driving her nuts!

Having Michiko had made her realize she had spent too much of her time demanding her impossible standards be met by all the men she knew but especially Kendrick just because of one person's actions and life was simply too precious to continue to waste her time that way. She truly loved Kendrick and wanted to spend to rest of her life with him. She prayed she hadn't realized too late. She had attempted to bring it up a few times, he however refused to discuss it. It seemed when she broke his heart that last time was truly the LAST TIME

"Marry me." She whispered softly if he wouldn't ask her she would ask him. Kendrick jerked like she struck him. He took Michiko from her once she was finished nursing and put her in her bassinet.   After making sure the newborn was settled he turned back to Raven.

"May I sit?" He motioned to the rocking chair close to the bed.   Raven looked at him hopefully before moving a blanket from the chair.   He sat in the rocking chair and leaned forward. "Raven, I am so grateful to you for having our daughter and honored you 'allowed' me to name her after my grandmother but none of that can change the pain you put me through because of your lack of faith in me. I continuously asked you to trust me that I wasn't like any other man, Raven I was in love with you period no strings, the past didn't matter, not to me at least but you just wouldn't or couldn't let it go. I know ideally you get married first and then have children but I guess that wasn't how it was intended to play out for us. To be good parents to our daughter we just have to respect each other."

Raven sat quietly for a moment before the tears fell down her face and dropped on her clasped hands. Taking a deep breath, she looked over at Kendrick sadly. "Well think about it so we can figure out how we do this with Michiko. I mean I will never keep her from you but you don't have to stay here with us anymore. I am able to get around pretty good from the c-section so whenever you're ready you can move back to your place."   She stood to put the blanket she was still clutching away, fighting the urge to break down sobbing. Well she pushed and pushed and got what she lied and said she wanted, to be left alone.

"Raven?"   He called her name softly. She squared her shoulders and set her face with a plastic watery smile.

"Yes?"   He moved from the rocking chair and stood in front of her taking both of his hands in his.

"Like I have said time and time again, you don't listen for shit unless it's what you want to hear."   She looked up at him confused.

"What do you mean?" She asked breathlessly and cautiously hopeful.

"All I said was as Michiko's parents, we needed to respect each other. I never once said in the sentence I didn't want to be with you." She felt him slide his ring on her finger. "Raven for the last damn time will you marry me?" She laughed and threw her arms around his neck.

"Hmm, let me think about it for a while." He picked her up and held her close in his arms.

"Damn that woman. You had your time to think, if was up to me we would be getting married today, as a matter of fact let me make some phone calls we could be married this weekend!"

Epilogue

The gong sounded to announce the beginning of the tea ceremony. Raven stood with Kendrick's assistance as she had Michiko cradled in her arms. The baby was dressed in white lace her parents both in white silk.   They entered to tea house hand in hand, matching wedding rings shining. They kneeled in front of elderly Japanese woman performing the ceremony after bowing, memories of his Kendrick's beloved grandmother filled her head. She gave up a prayer of thanks. With her husband by her side and her daughter in arms she finally felt at peace with who she was. Who she was as a physician, as a mother and now a wife but most importantly who she was as a woman. It no longer mattered how *she began that journey but how she now lived it.*